Jean Ingelow

Favorite Poems

Jean Ingelow

Favorite Poems

ISBN/EAN: 9783337206567

Printed in Europe, USA, Canada, Australia, Japan

Cover: Foto ©Andreas Hilbeck / pixelio.de

More available books at **www.hansebooks.com**

Very sincerely yours
Jean Ingelow

FAVORITE POEMS.

BY JEAN INGELOW.

SONGS OF SEVEN.   THE HIGH TIDE.

THE SHEPHERD LADY,

AND OTHER POEMS.

Illustrated.

BOSTON:
ROBERTS BROTHERS.
1886.

University Press:
JOHN WILSON AND SON, CAMBRIDGE.

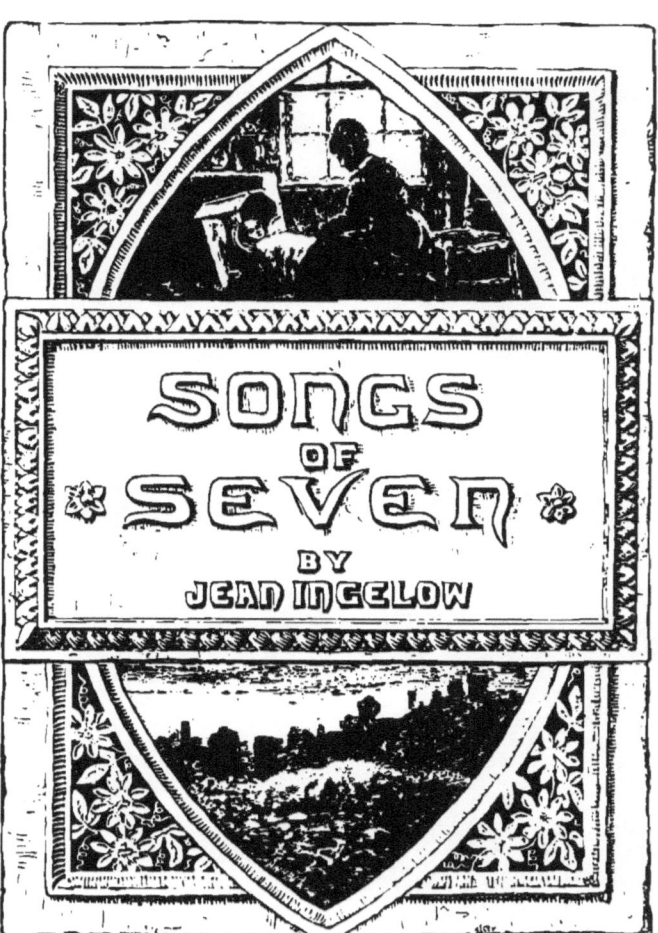

SONGS
OF
SEVEN
BY
JEAN INGELOW

SONGS OF SEVEN.

BY

JEAN INGELOW.

Illustrated.

BOSTON:
ROBERTS BROTHERS.
1886.

The full-page illustrations are designed by Miss C. A. NORTHAM and J. FRANCIS MURPHY; the titlepage, and those in the text, by EDMUND H. GARRETT. The book is prepared and the illustrations engraved by GEO. T. ANDREW.

CONTENTS

SEVEN TIMES ONE.

EXULTATION.

EXULTATION.

"I am seven times one to-day."

SONGS OF SEVEN.

—·—

Seven times One.

EXULTATION.

THERE'S no dew left on the daisies and
    clover
  There's no rain left in heaven;
I've said my "seven times" over and over,
  Seven times one are seven.

  I am old, so old, I can write a letter;
    My birthday lessons are done;
  The lambs play always, they know no better;
    They are only one times one.

O moon! in the night I have seen you sailing
 And shining so round and low;
You were bright! ah bright! but your light is
   failing:
 You are nothing now but a bow

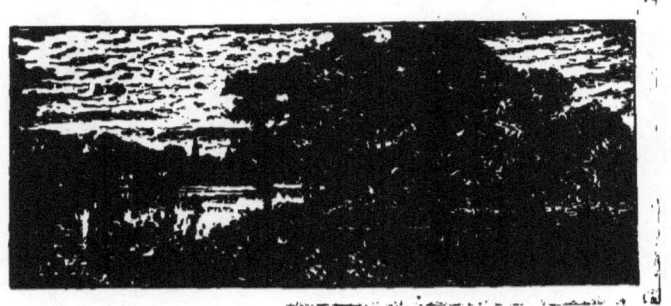

You moon, have you done something wrong in
   heaven
 That God has hidden your face?
I hope if you have you will soon be forgiven,
 And shine again in your place.

O velvet bee, you're a dusty fellow,
 You've powdered your legs with gold!
O brave marsh marybuds, rich and yellow,
 Give me your money to hold!

O columbine, open your folded wrapper,
  Where two twin turtle-doves dwell!
O cuckoopint, toll me the purple clapper
  That hangs in your clear green bell.

And show me your nest with the young
          ones in it;
  I will not steal them away;
I am old! you may trust me, linnet, linnet:
  I am seven times one to-day.

SEVEN TIMES TWO.

———•———

ROMANCE.

ROMANCE.

"I went for my story — the birds cannot sing it."

Seven times Two.

ROMANCE.

YOU bells in the steeple, ring, ring out your
    changes,
  How many soever they be,
And let the brown meadow-lark's note as he
    ranges
  Come over, come over to me.

Yet bird's clearest carol by fall or by swelling
  No magical sense conveys,
And bells have forgotten their old art of telling
  The fortune of future days.

"Turn again, turn again," once they rang cheerily,
   While a boy listened alone;
Made his heart yearn again, musing so wearily
   All by himself on a stone.

Poor bells! I forgive you; your good days are over,
   And mine, they are yet to be;
No listening, no longing, shall aught, aught discover:
   You leave the story to me.

The foxglove shoots out of the green matted heather,
   Preparing her hoods of snow;
She was idle, and slept till the sunshiny weather:
   O children take long to grow.

I wish, and I wish that the spring would go faster,
  Nor long summer bide so late;
And I could grow on like the foxglove and aster,
  For some things are ill to wait.

I wait for the day when dear hearts shall discover,
  While dear hands are laid on my head;
"The child is a woman, the book may close over,
  For all the lessons are said."

I wait for my story — the birds cannot sing it,
  Not one, as he sits on the tree;
The bells cannot ring it, but long years, O bring it!
  Such as I wish it to be.

SEVEN TIMES THREE.

—•—

LOVE.

Seven times Three.

LOVE.

I LEANED out of window, I smelt the white
clover,
Dark, dark was the garden, I saw not the gate;
"Now, if there be footsteps, he comes, my one
lover —
Hush, nightingale, hush! O, sweet nightingale,
wait
Till I listen and hear
If a step draweth near,
For my love he is late!

" The skies in the darkness stoop nearer and nearer,
   A cluster of stars hangs like fruit in the tree,
The fall of the water comes sweeter, comes clearer:
   To what art thou listening, and what dost thou see?
      Let the star-clusters glow,
      Let the sweet waters flow,
      And cross quickly to me.

" You night-moths that hover where honey brims
     over
   From sycamore blossoms, or settle or sleep:
You glow-worms, shine out, and the pathway dis-
     cover
   To him that comes darkling along the rough steep.
      Ah, my sailor, make haste,
      For the time runs to waste,
      And my love lieth deep —

" Too deep for swift telling; and yet, my one lover
   I've conned thee an answer, it waits thee to-night."
By the sycamore passed he, and through the white
      clover,
   Then all the sweet speech I had fashioned took
      flight;
            But I'll love him more, more
            Than e'er wife loved before,
            Be the days dark or bright.

SEVEN TIMES FOUR.

---·---

MATERNITY.

MATERNITY.

"Heigh-ho! daisies and buttercups!
Mother shall thread them a daisy chain."

Seven times Four.

MATERNITY.

HEIGH-HO! daisies and buttercups,
  Fair yellow daffodils, stately and tall!
When the wind wakes how they rock in the grasses,
  And dance with the cuckoo-buds slender and
    small!
Here's two bonny boys, and here's mother's own
    lasses,
        Eager to gather them all.

Heigh-ho! daisies and buttercups!
    Mother shall thread them a daisy chain;
Sing them a song of the pretty hedge-sparrow,
    That loved her brown little ones, loved them
        full fain;
Sing, " Heart, thou art wide though the house be
    but narrow," —
        Sing once, and sing it again.

Heigh-ho! daisies and buttercups,
    Sweet wagging cowslips, they bend and they bow;
A ship sails afar over warm ocean waters,
    And haply one musing doth stand at her prow.
O bonny brown sons, and O sweet little daughters,
        Maybe he thinks on you now!

Heigh-ho! daisies and buttercups,
    Fair yellow daffodils, stately and tall —
A sunshiny world full of laughter and leisure,
    And fresh hearts unconscious of sorrow and thrall!
Send down on their pleasure smiles passing its meas-
       ure,
           God that is over us all!

SEVEN TIMES FIVE.

WIDOWHOOD.

WIDOWHOOD.

"I lift mine eyes, and what to
But a too soft happy and two"

Seven times Five.

WIDOWHOOD.

I SLEEP and rest, my heart makes
 moan
 Before I am well awake:
"Let me bleed! O let me alone,
 Since I must not break!"

For children wake, though fathers
 sleep
 With a stone at foot and at head:
O sleepless God, for ever keep,
 Keep both living and dead!

I lift mine eyes, and what to see
  But a world happy and fair!
I have not wished it to mourn with
      me,—
  Comfort is not there.

O what anear but golden brooms,
  And a waste of reedy rills!
O what afar but the fine glooms
  On the rare blue hills!

    I shall not die, but live forlore
      How bitter it is to part!
    O to meet thee, my love, once more!
      O my heart, my heart!

No more to hear, no more to see!
   O that an echo might wake
And waft one note of thy psalm to me
   Ere my heart strings break!

            I should know it how faint soe'er,
               And with angel-voices blent;
            O once to feel thy spirit anear,
               I could be content.

Or once between the gates of gold,
   While an entering angel trod,
But once — thee sitting to behold
   On the hills of God!

SEVEN TIMES SIX.

GIVING IN MARRIAGE.

GIVING IN MARRIAGE.

"'Tis m Co   t at you serve me Ald,
Tis ja   ins so than."

Seven times Six.

GIVING IN MARRIAGE.

TO bear, to nurse, to rear,
    To watch, and then to lose :
To see my bright ones disappear,
    Drawn up like morning dews—
To bear, to nurse, to rear,
    To watch, and then to lose :
This have I done when God drew
        near
    Among his own to choose.

To hear, to heed, to wed,
    And with thy lord depart
In tears that he, as soon as shed,
    Will let no longer smart. —
To hear, to heed, to wed,
    This while thou didst I smiled,
For now it was not God who said,
    " Mother, give ME thy child."

O fond, O fool, and blind,
    To God I gave with tears;
But when a man like grace would find,
    My soul put by her fears.
O fond, O fool, and blind,
    God guards in happier spheres;
That man will guard where he did bind
    Is hope for unknown years.

To hear, to heed, to wed,
    Fair lot that maidens choose,
Thy mother's tenderest words are said,
    Thy face no more she views;
Thy mother's lot, my dear,
    She doth in naught accuse;
Her lot to bear, to nurse, to rear,
    To love — and then to lose.

SEVEN TIMES SEVEN.

———•———

LONGING FOR HOME.

LONGING FOR HOME.

"Can I call that home where I anchor yet,
Though my good man has sailed?"

Seven times Seven.

LONGING FOR HOME.

A SONG of a boat: —
　　There was once a boat on a billow:
Lightly she rocked to her port remote,
　　And the foam was white in her wake like snow,
And her frail mast bowed when the breeze would
　　　　blow,
　　And bent like a wand of willow.

I shaded mine eyes one day when a boat
    Went curtseying over the billow,
I marked her course till a dancing mote
She faded out on the moonlit foam,
And I stayed behind in the dear loved home;
    And my thoughts all day were about the boat,
    And my dreams upon the pillow.

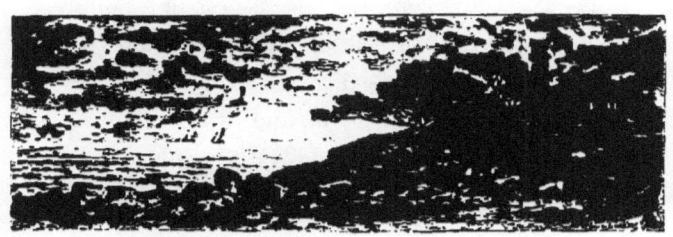

I pray you hear my song of a boat,
    For it is but short : —
My boat, you shall find none fairer afloat,
    In river or port.
Long I looked out for the lad she bore,
    On the open desolate sea,
And I think he sailed to the heavenly shore,
    For he came not back to me —
                        Ah me!

A song of a nest : —
  There was once a nest in a hollow :
Down in the mosses and knot-grass
  pressed,
  Soft and warm, and full to the brim.
  Vetches leaned over it purple and dim,
  With buttercup buds to follow.

I pray you hear my song of a nest,
  For it is not long : —
You shall never light, in a summer quest
  The bushes among —
Shall never light on a prouder sitter,
  A fairer nestful, nor ever know
A softer sound than their tender twitter,
  That wind-like did come and go.

I had a nestful once of my own,
    Ah happy, happy I !
Right dearly I loved them : but when they
    were grown
    They spread out their wings to fly.
O, one after one they flew away
    Far up to the heavenly blue,
To the better country, the upper day,
    And — I wish I was going too.

I pray you, what is the nest to me,
    My empty nest ?
And what is the shore where I stood to see
    My boat sail down to the west ?
Can I call that home where I anchor yet,
    Though my good man has sailed ?

Can I call that home where my nest was set,
    Now all its hope hath failed?
Nay, but the port where my sailor went,
    And the land where my nestlings be, —
There is the home where my thoughts are sent
    The only home for me —
                        Ah me!

The·High·Tide· on the coast of Lincolnshire· ·1571·

THE HIGH TIDE ON THE COAST OF LINCOLNSHIRE 1571 by Jean Ingelow

PUBLISHED BY ROBERTS BROTHERS OF BOSTON IN THE STATE OF MASSACHUSETTS A.D. MDCCCLXXXIII

JOHN WILSON & SON.

UNIVERSITY PRESS.

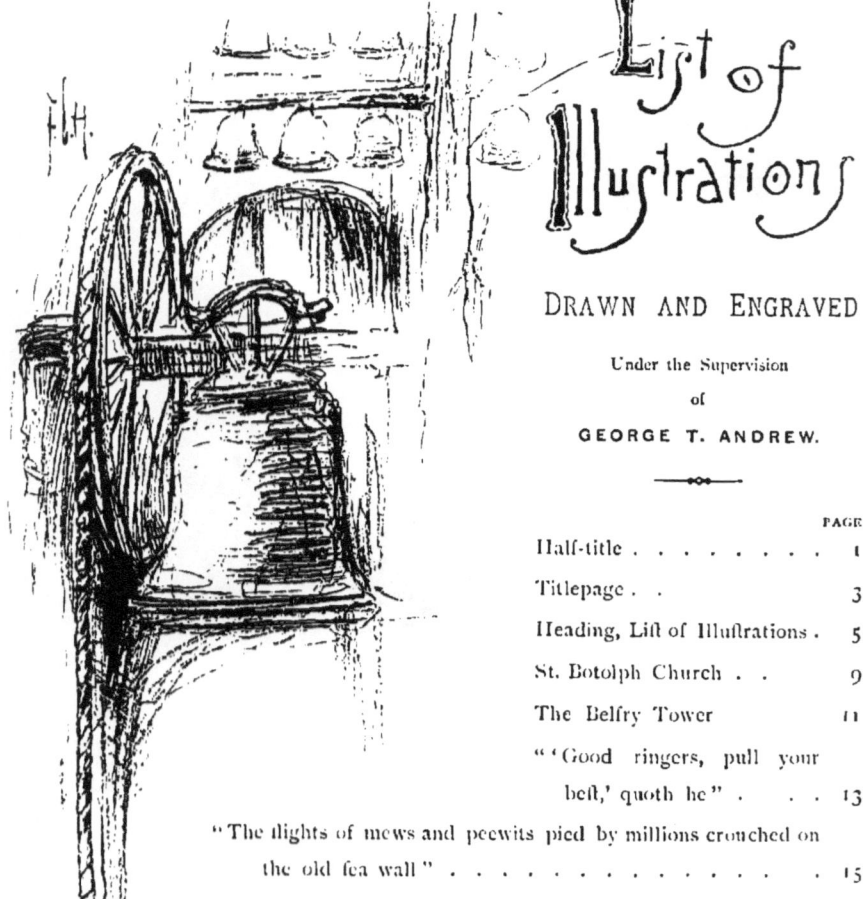

List of Illustrations

DRAWN AND ENGRAVED

Under the Supervision

of

GEORGE T. ANDREW.

Illustrations in Notes.

ARTISTS.

F. S. CHURCH. WM. ST. JOHN HARPER.

HARRY FENN. J. APPLETON BROWN.

W. A. ROGERS. F. B. SCHELL.

J. FRANCIS MURPHY. W. F. HALSALL.

J. D. WOODWARD. W. L. TAYLOR.

F. CHILDE HASSAM.

SEAL.
OLD BOSTON, ENGLAND.

St. Botolph Church.

The High Tide.

THE old mayor climbed the belfry tower,
 The ringers rang by two, by three;
" Pull, if ye never pulled before;
 Good ringers, pull your beſt," quoth he.
" Play uppe, play uppe, O Boſton bells!
Ply all your changes, all your ſwells,
 Play uppe ' The Brides of Enderby.' "

"'Good ringers, pull your best,' quoth he."

Men fay it was a ftolen tyde —

    The Lord that fent it, He knows all;

But in myne ears doth ftill abide

    The meffage that the bells let fall:

    And there was nought of ftrange, befide

    The flights of mews and peewits pied

    By millions crouched on the old fea wall.

I fat and fpun within the doore,
  My thread brake off, I raifed myne eyes;

The level fun, like ruddy ore,
  Lay finking in the barren fkies;
And dark againft day's golden death
She moved where Lindis wandereth,
  My fonne's faire wife, Elizabeth.

"Cufha! Cufha! Cufha!" calling,
Ere the early dews were falling,
Farre away I heard her fong,
"Cufha! Cufha!" all along;
Where the reedy Lindis floweth,
        Floweth, floweth,
From the meads where melick groweth
Faintly came her milking fong —

"My sonne's faire wife, Elizabeth."

"Cuſha! Cuſha! Cuſha!" calling,
" For the dews will ſoone be falling;
Leave your meadow graſſes mellow,
   Mellow, mellow;
   Quit your cowſlips, cowſlips yellow;
   Come uppe Whitefoot, come uppe Lightfoot;
   Quit the ſtalks of parſley hollow,
     Hollow, hollow;

   Come uppe Jetty, riſe and follow,
   From the clovers lift your head;
   Come uppe Whitefoot, come uppe Lightfoot,
   Come uppe Jetty, riſe and follow,
   Jetty, to the milking ſhed."

If it be long, ay, long ago,
   When I beginne to think howe long,
Againe I hear the Lindis flow,
   Swift as an arrowe, ſharpe and ſtrong ;
And all the aire, it ſeemeth mee,
Bin full of floating bells (ſayth thee),
That ring the tune of Enderby.

Alle frefh the level pafture lay,
 And not a fhadowe mote be feene,
Save where full fyve good miles away
 The fteeple towered from out the greene ;
And lo ! the great bell farre and wide
Was heard in all the country fide
That Saturday at eventide.

The fwanherds where their fedges are
 Moved on in funfet's golden breath,
The fhepherde lads I heard afarre,
 And my fonne's wife, Elizabeth ;
Till floating o'er the graffy fea
Came downe that kyndly meffage free,
The " Brides of Mavis Enderby."

Then fome looked uppe into the fky,

And all along where Lindis flows

To where the goodly veffels lie,

And where the lordly fteeple fhows.

They fayde, "And why fhould this thing be?

What danger lowers by land or fea?

They ring the tune of Enderby!

" For evil news from Mablethorpe,

   Of pyrate galleys warping down ;

For fhippes afhore beyond the fcorpe,

   They have not fpared to wake the towne :

But while the weft bin red to fee,

And ftorms be none, and pyrates flee,

Why ring ' The Brides of Enderby ' ? "

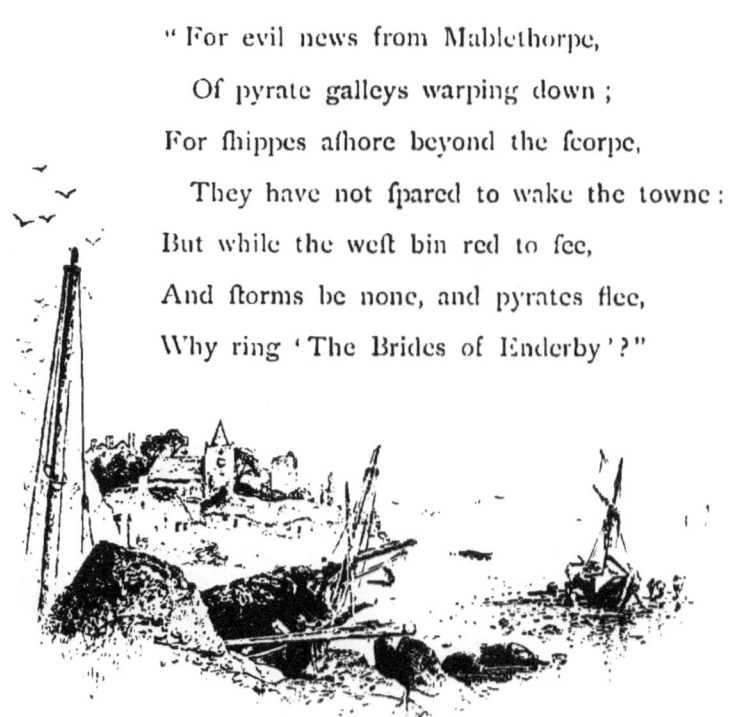

" Of pyrate galleys warping down."

I looked without, and lo! my fonne
   Came riding downe with might and main :
He raifed a fhout as he drew on,
   Till all the welkin rang again,
"Elizabeth ! Elizabeth !"
(A fweeter woman ne'er drew breath
Than my fonne's wife, Elizabeth.)

"The old fea wall," he cried, "is downe.
   The rifing tide comes on apace,
And boats adrift in yonder towne
   Go failing uppe the market-place."
He fhook as one that looks on death :
"God fave you, mother !" ftraight he faith ;
"Where is my wife, Elizabeth ?"

"Good fonne, where Lindis winds away,
   With her two bairns I marked her long ;
And ere yon bells beganne to play
   Afar I heard her milking fong."
He looked acrofs the graffy lea,
To right, to left, " Ho, Enderby ! "
They rang " The Brides of Enderby ! "

With that he cried and beat his breaſt;
  For, lo! along the river's bed
A mighty eygre reared his creſt,
  And uppe the Lindis raging ſped.
It ſwept with thunderous noiſes loud;
Shaped like a curling ſnow-white cloud,
Or like a demon in a ſhroud.

And rearing Lindis backward preſſed,
  Shook all her trembling bankes amaine;
Then madly at the eygre's breaſt
  Flung uppe her weltering walls again.
Then bankes came downe with ruin and rout —
Then beaten foam flew round about —
Then all the mighty floods were out.

"Then beaten foam flew round about –
Then all the mighty floods were out."

So farre, fo faft the eygre drave,
  The heart had hardly time to beat,
Before a fhallow feething wave

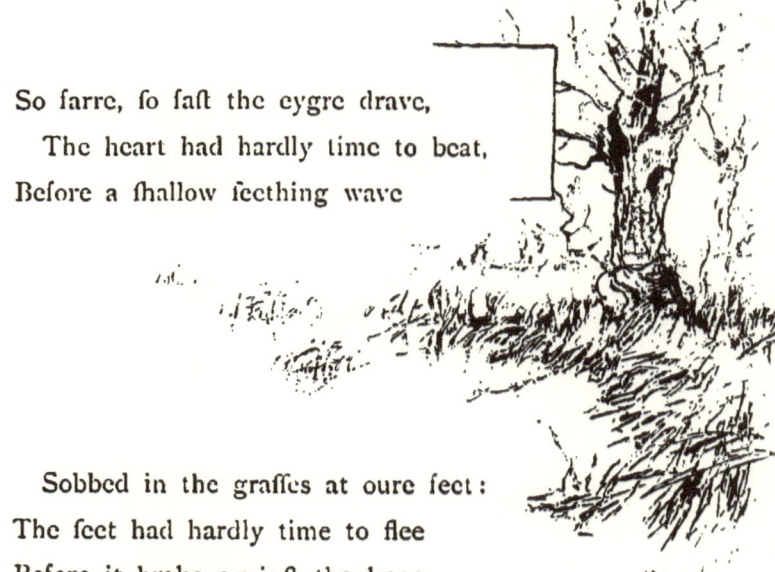

  Sobbed in the graffes at oure feet:
The feet had hardly time to flee
Before it brake againft the knee,
And all the world was in the fea.

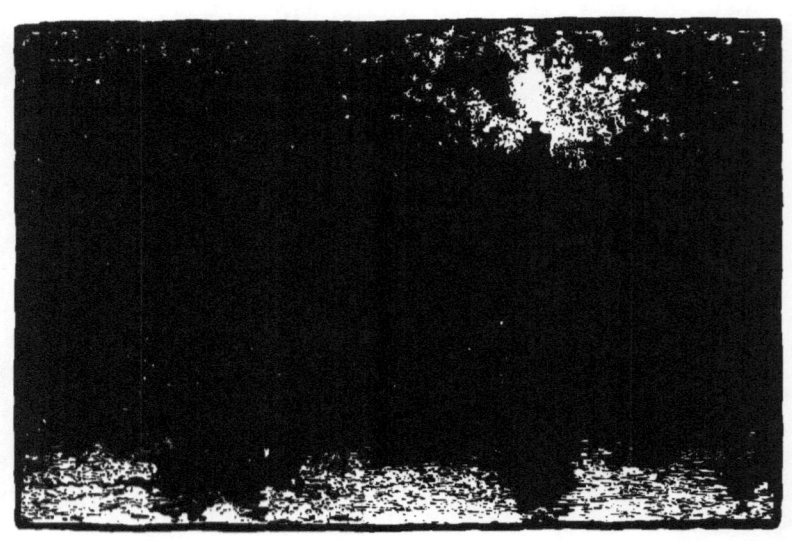

Upon the roofe we fate that night,
 The noife of bells went fweeping by ;
I marked the lofty beacon light
Stream from the church tower, red and high —
A lurid mark and dread to fee ;
And awfome bells they were to mee,
That in the dark rang " Enderby."

They rang the failor lads to guide

From roofe to roofe who fearlefs rowed;

And I — my fonne was at my fide,

And yet the ruddy beacon glowed;

And yet he moaned beneath his breath,

"O come in life, or come in death!

O loft! my love, Elizabeth."

" *Upon the roofe we fate that night.*"

And didſt thou viſit him no more?
  Thou didſt, thou didſt, my daughter deare;
The waters laid thee at his doore,
  Ere yet the early dawn was clear.
Thy pretty bairns in faſt embrace,
The lifted ſun ſhone on thy face,
Downe drifted to thy dwelling-place.

That flow ftrewed wrecks about the grafs,

That ebbe fwept out the flocks to fea;

A fatal ebbe and flow, alas!
  To manye more than myne and mee:
But each will mourn his own (the faith).
And fweeter woman ne'er drew breath
Than my fonne's wife, Elizabeth.

I fhall never hear her more
By the reedy Lindis fhore,
" Cufha! Cufha! Cufha!" calling,
Ere the early dews be falling ;
I fhall never hear her fong,
" Cufha! Cufha!" all along
Where the funny Lindis floweth,
    Goeth, floweth ;
From the meads where melick groweth,
When the water winding down,
Onward floweth to the town.

"'Cusha! Cusha! Cusha!' calling."

I shall never see her more
Where the reeds and rushes quiver,
Shiver, quiver;

Stand beside the sobbing river,
Sobbing, throbbing, in its falling
To the sandy lonesome shore;

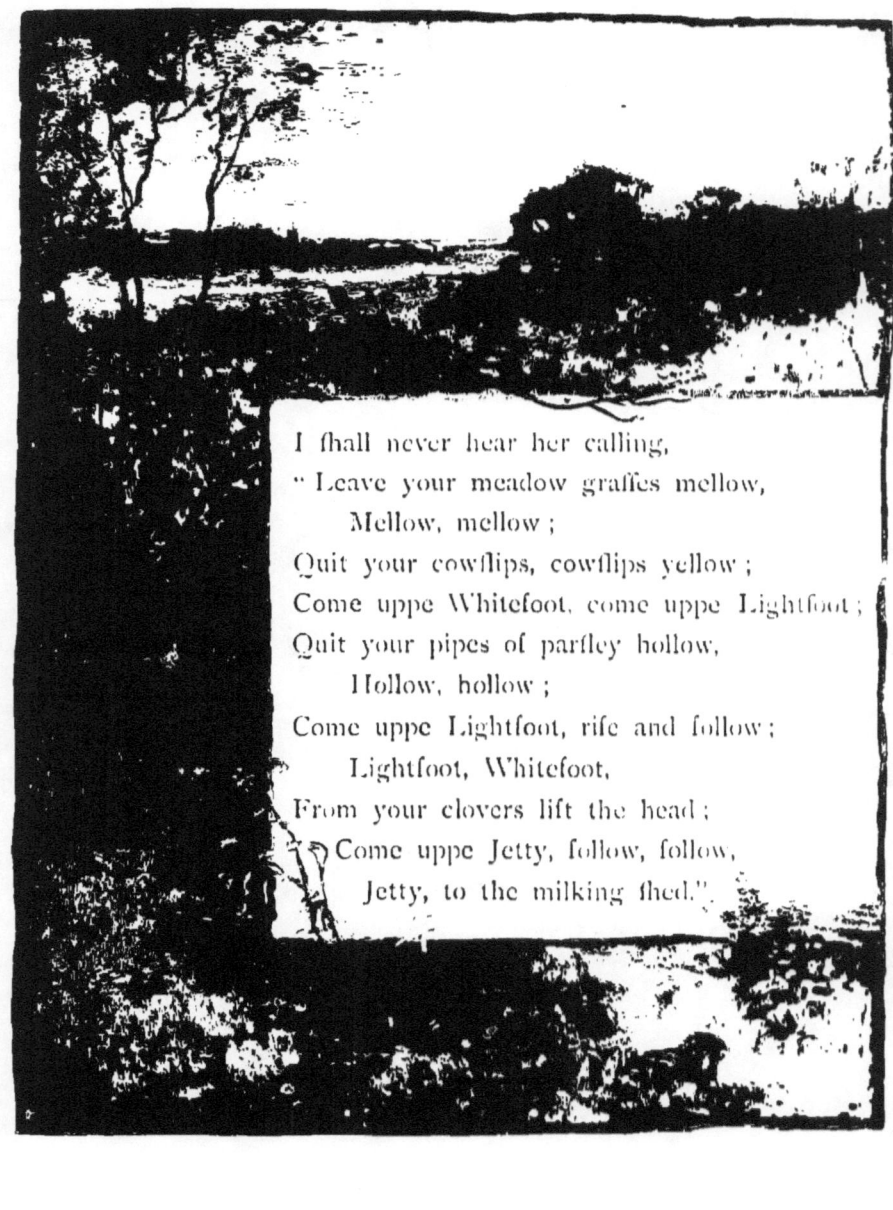

I ſhall never hear her calling,
" Leave your meadow graſſes mellow,
      Mellow, mellow ;
Quit your cowſlips, cowſlips yellow ;
Come uppe Whitefoot, come uppe Lightfoot ;
Quit your pipes of parſley hollow,
      Hollow, hollow ;
Come uppe Lightfoot, rife and follow ;
      Lightfoot, Whitefoot,
From your clovers lift the head ;
Come uppe Jetty, follow, follow,
      Jetty, to the milking ſhed."

"But each will mourn his own."

JEAN INGELOW'S HOME.

JEAN INGELOW, the author of "The High Tide on the Coast of Lincoln shire," was born in the quaint old city of Boston, under the shadow of St. Botolph's tower. Writing of her childish days, she says: "We had a lofty nursery, with a bow-window" (which can be seen in the picture) "that overlooked the river. My brother and I were constantly wondering at this river. The coming up of the tides, and the ships, and the jolly gangs of towers dragging them on with a monotonous song, made a daily delight for us." At this time she was three years old, and in one of her poems she sings of "The days without alloy:" —

> "When I sit on market-days amid the comers and the goers,
>   Oh! full oft I have a vision of the days without alloy,
>   And a ship comes up the river with a jolly gang of towers,
>   And a 'pull' e haul' e, pull' e haul' e, yoy! heave, hoy!'"

NOTE I. — PAGE 11.

"The old mayor climbed the belfry tower."

THE bells at Boston were always rung on occasions of danger, and the belfry tower of St. Botolph Church was the only height from which could be seen the country around and out to the sea. It was a great beacon, and the top was a lanthorn-tower, supporting a lanthorn three hundred feet high in air, visible at sea for forty miles, which was lighted at night on such occasions, and to guide people to the town; for the country was one vast pasture, with no high-roads between Boston and the sea. So the mayor and the ringers, on receiving news of the great tide coming in, "climbed the belfry tower."

NOTE II. — PAGE 11.

" O Boston Bells ! "

In the seventh century a pious monk, known as St. Botolph, or Bot-holp, i. e. Boathelp, founded a church at a place called Y-cean-ho. The town which grew up around it was called Botolph's Town, contracted into Bot'-olphston, Bot'-os-ton, and finally *Boston*. "Botolphstowne standeth hard on ye river of Lindis. The steeple of the church ' being *quadrata Turris* ' and a lanthorn on it, is both very high and faire, and a marke bothe by sea and land, for all ye quarters thereaboute. The stream of it is sometymes as swift as it were an arrow. The mayne se ys VI. miles of Boston. Dyverse good shipps, and other vessells ryde there." (From an account written in 1541.)

NOTE III. — PAGE 11.

" Play uppe ' The Brides of Enderby.' "

It is said that the people knew by the language of the bells what was the occasion of their ringing, the different peals meaning different things.

NOTE IV. — PAGE 15.

" Men say it was a stolen tyde."

A "stolen tyde" was meant to express a tide which rose at full of the moon, or in moderately calm weather, to an unprecedented height, — stole upon the country, as it were, and was not the result of great wind and storm. The poem is intended to convey the idea that there was a calm sunset, no commotion in the elements, and hence the surprise of the country people, who when they heard an alarm-peal did not at first know why they were warned.

Note V. — Page 17.

"*She moved where Lindis wandereth.*"

The name of the river on which the town of Boston is situated, — an abbreviation of Lindissey, which also is an abbreviation of Lincolnshire.

Note VI. — Page 33.

"*For evil news from Mablethorpe.*"

An adjoining parish, which suffered terribly from the devastation of the high tide in 1571.

SKIRBECK CHURCH, BOSTON, ENGLAND.

This church stood on the brink of the river, at the time of the disaster consequent upon the high tide. When a child Miss Ingelow always attended service in this church.

NOTE VII. — PAGE 41.

" *A mighty eygre reared his crest.*"

An *eygre* is the great wave which, when the tide turns, rushes up a tidal river that is pent in between high rocks or artificial banks, and, meeting the fresh water coming down, causes devastation and disaster. In the case of the high tide of 1571 it burst the banks of the river, tore down the "old sea-wall," which was another bank, and flooded the country.

THE OLD VICARAGE, BOSTON, ENGLAND.

In this vicarage the Rev. John Cotton lived whilst he was vicar, before he fled to Boston, New England. John Cotton was born at Derby, 4th Dec. 1585; entered Trinity College, 1598; appointed to the vicarage of Boston, England, 1612; compelled to resign because he was guilty of Puritanism and Nonconformity, 1633; arrived at Boston, New England, 4th Sept. 1633; ordained 16th Oct. 1633, over the First Church in *New* Boston; died 23d Dec. 1652; and on the 29th of that month he was carried on the shoulders of his fellow-ministers to the burial-ground of King's Chapel.

SHEPHERD LADY,

AND OTHER POEMS.

By JEAN INGELOW,
AUTHOR OF "SONGS OF SEVEN."

BOSTON:

ROBERTS BROTHERS.

1886.

CONTENTS.

LIST OF ILLUSTRATIONS.

THE ENGRAVINGS BY LINTON, ANTHONY, DALZIEL BROTHERS, AND JOHN ANDREW AND SON (UNDER WHOSE SUPERVISION THEY ARE PRINTED).

———— •

THE SHEPHERD LADY.

I.

WHO pipes upon the long green hill,
    Where meadow grass is deep?
The white lamb bleats but followeth on —
    Follow the clean white sheep.
The dear white lady in yon high tower,
    She hearkeneth in her sleep.

All in long grass the piper stands,
    Goodly and grave is he;
Outside the tower, at dawn of day,
    The notes of his pipe ring free.
A thought from his heart doth reach to hers:
    "Come down, O lady! to me."

The Shepherd Lady.

She lifts her head, she dons her gown :
    Ah ! the lady is fair ;
She ties the girdle on her waist,
    And binds her flaxen hair,
And down she stealeth, down and down,
    Down the turret stair.

Behold him ! With the flock he wons
    Along yon grassy lea.
" My shepherd lord, my shepherd love,
    What wilt thou, then, with me ?
My heart is gone out of my breast,
    And followeth on to thee."

"The dear white lady in yon high tower,
She lieth in her sleep."

II.

" The white lambs feed in tender grass :
　With them and thee to bide,
How good it were," she saith at noon ;
　" Albeit the meads are wide.
Oh ! well is me," she saith when day
　Draws on to eventide.

Hark ! hark ! the shepherd's voice.　Oh, sweet !
　Her tears drop down like rain.
" Take now this crook, my chosen, my fere,
　And tend the flock full fain ;
Feed them, O lady, and lose not one,
　Till I shall come again."

Right soft her speech : " My will is thine,
　And my reward thy grace ! "
Gone are his footsteps over the hill,
　Withdrawn his goodly face ;
The mournful dusk begins to gather,
　The daylight wanes apace.

"Take now this crook."

The Shepherd Lady.

III.

On sunny slopes, ah! long the lady
    Feedeth her flock at noon ;
She leads it down to drink at eve
    Where the small rivulets croon.
All night her locks are wet with dew,
    Her eyes outwatch the moon.

Beyond the hills her voice is heard,
    She sings when light doth wane :
" My longing heart is full of love,
    Nor shall my watch be vain.
My shepherd lord, I see him not,
    But he will come again."

"On sunny slopes, and long the bray
Feedeth her flock at noon

ABOVE THE CLOUDS.

A ND can this be my own world?
      'Tis all gold and snow,
Save where scarlet waves are hurled
   Down yon gulf below?
'Tis thy world, 'tis my world,
   City, mead, and shore,
For he that hath his own world
   Hath many worlds more.

LOVE'S THREAD OF GOLD.

IN the night she told a story,
   In the night and all night through,
While the moon was in her glory,
   And the branches dropped with dew.
'Twas my life she told, and round it
   Rose the years as from a deep;
In the world's great heart she found it,
   Cradled like a child asleep.
In the night I saw her weaving
   By the misty moonbeam cold,
All the weft her shuttle cleaving
   With a sacred thread of gold.
Ah! she wept me tears of sorrow,
   Lulling tears so mystic sweet;
Then she wove my last to-morrow,
   And her web lay at my feet.

Love's Thread of Gold.

Of my life she made the story :
  I must weep — so soon 'twas told !
But your name did lend it glory,
  And your love its thread of gold !

FAILURE.

WE are much bound to them that do succeed ;
   But, in a more pathetic sense, are bound
To such as fail. They all our loss expound ;
They comfort us for work that will not speed,
And life — itself a failure.

Failure.

Ay, his deed,
Sweetest in story, who the dusk profound
Of Hades flooded with entrancing sound,
Music's own tears, was failure. Doth it read
Therefore the worse? Ah, no! so much to dare,

He fronts the regnant Darkness on its throne. —
So much to do; impetuous even there,

He pours out love's disconsolate sweet moan —
He wins; but few for that his deed recall:
Its power is in the look which costs him all.

ONE MORNING, OH! SO EARLY.

ONE morning, oh! so early, my belovèd, my belovèd,
   All the birds were singing blithely, as if never they
      would cease ;
'Twas a thrush sang in my garden, "Hear the story, hear the
   story!"
         And the lark sang, "Give us glory!"
         And the dove said, "Give us peace!"

Then I listened, oh! so early, my belovèd, my belovèd,
To that murmur from the woodland of the dove, my dear, the
   dove ;
When the nightingale came after, "Give us fame to sweeten
   duty!"
         When the wren sang, "Give us beauty!"
         She made answer, "Give us love!"

24

One Morning, Oh! So Early.

Sweet is spring, and sweet the morning, my belovèd, my
   belovèd ;
Now for us doth spring, doth morning, wait upon the year's
   increase,
And my prayer goes up, " Oh, give us, crowned in youth with
   marriage glory,
         Give for all our life's dear story,
         Give us love, and give us peace ! "

THE DAYS WITHOUT ALLOY.

WHEN I sit on market-days amid the comers and the
goers,
  Oh! full oft I have a vision of the days without alloy,
And a ship comes up the river with a jolly gang of towers,
  And a "pull'e haul'e, pull'e haul'e, yoy! heave, hoy!"

There is busy talk around me, all about mine ears it hummeth,
  But the wooden wharves I look on, and a dancing, heaving
    buoy,
For 'tis tidetime in the river, and she cometh — oh, she
    cometh!
  With a "pull'e haul'e, pull'e haul'e, yoy! heave, hoy!"

Then I hear the water washing, never golden waves were
  brighter,
  And I hear the capstan creaking — 'tis a sound that cannot
    cloy.

" And a ship comes up the river with a jolly gang of towers."

The Days Without Alloy.

Bring her to, to ship her lading, brig or schooner, sloop or
    lighter,
  With a "pull'e haul'e, pull'e haul'e, yoy! heave, hoy!"

"Will ye step aboard, my dearest? for the high seas lie be-
    fore us."
  So I sailed with him the river in those days without alloy;
Sailed afar, but when, I wonder, shall a sweeter sound float
    o'er us
  Than yon "pull'e haul'e, pull'e haul'e, yoy! heave, hoy!"

THE LEAVES OF LIGN ALOES.

DROP, drop from the leaves of lign aloes,
　　O honey-dew! drop from the tree.
Float up through your clear river shallows,
　　White lilies, beloved of the bee.

Let the people, O Queen! say, and bless thee,
　　Her bounty drops soft as the dew,
And spotless in honor confess thee,
　　As lilies are spotless in hue.

On the roof stands yon white stork awaking,
　　His feathers flush rosy the while,
For, lo! from the blushing east breaking,
　　The sun sheds the bloom of his smile.

Let them boast of thy word. " It is certain ;
　　We doubt it no more," let them say,
" Than to-morrow that night's dusky curtain
　　Shall roll back its folds for the day."

29

ON THE ROCKS BY ABERDEEN.

ON the rocks by Aberdeen,
　　Where the whislin' wave had been,
As I wandered and at e'en
　　Was eerie;
There I saw thee sailing west,
And I ran with joy opprest —
Ay, and took out all my best,
　　My dearie.

Then I busked mysel' wi' speed,
And the neighbors cried " What need ?
'Tis a lass in any weed
　　Aye bonny ! "
Now my heart, my heart is sair:
What's the good, though I be fair,
For thou'lt never see me mair,
　　Man Johnnie !

" Then I busked mysel' wi' speed,
And the neighbors cried " What need ?"

FEATHERS AND MOSS.

THE marten flew to the finch's nest,
    Feathers and moss, and a wisp of hay:
"The arrow it sped to thy brown mate's breast;
    Low in the broom is thy mate to-day."

"Liest thou low, love? low in the broom?
    Feathers and moss, and a wisp of hay,
Warm the white eggs till I learn his doom."
    She beateth her wings, and away, away.

"Ah, my sweet singer, thy days are told
    (Feathers and moss, and a wisp of hay)!
Thine eyes are dim, and the eggs grow cold.
    O mournful morrow! O dark to-day!"

The finch flew back to her cold, cold nest,
    Feathers and moss, and a wisp of hay,
Mine is the trouble that rent her breast,
    And home is silent, and love is clay.

S WEET is childhood — childhood's over,
    Kiss and part.
Sweet is youth; but youth's a rover —
    So's my heart.
Sweet is rest; but by all showing
    Toil is nigh.
We must go. Alas! the going,
    Say "good-bye."

THE GYPSY'S SELLING SONG.

M Y good man — he's an old, old man,
And my good man got a fall,
To buy me a bargain so fast he ran
When he heard the gypsies call:
"Buy, buy brushes,
Baskets wrought o' rushes.
Buy them, buy them, take them, try them,
Buy, dames all."

My old man, he has money and land,
And a young, young wife am I.
Let him put the penny in my white hand
When he hears the gypsies cry:
"Buy, buy laces,
Veils to screen your faces.
Buy them, buy them, take and try them.
Buy, maids, buy."

" Buy them, buy them, take and try them.
Buy, maids, buy."

MY FAIR LADY.

M Y fair lady's a dear, dear lady —
　　I walked by her side to woo.
In a garden alley, so sweet and shady,
　　She answered, " I love not you,
　　　　John, John Brady,"
　　　　Quoth my dear lady,
" Pray now, pray now, go your way now,
　　　　Do, John, do ! "

Yet my fair lady's my own, own lady,
　　For I passed another day ;
While making her moan, she sat all alone,
　　And thus and thus did she say :
　　　　" John, John Brady,"
　　　　Quoth my dear lady,
" Do now, do now, once more woo now,
　　　　Pray, John, pray ! "

SLEEP AND TIME.

"WAKE, baillie, wake! the crafts are out;
  Wake!" said the knight, "be quick!
For high street, bye street, over the town
  They fight with poker and stick."
Said the squire, "A fight so fell was ne'er
  In all thy bailliewick."
What said the old clock in the tower?
      "Tick, tick, tick!"

"Wake, daughter, wake! the hour draws on;
  Wake!" quoth the dame, "be quick!
The meats are set, the guests are coming,
  The fiddler waxing his stick."
She said, "The bridegroom waiting and waiting
  To see thy face is sick."
What said the new clock in her bower?
      "Tick, tick, tick!"

MASTER, QUOTH THE AULD HOUND.

"**M**ASTER," quoth the auld hound,
   "Where will ye go?"
"Over moss, over muir,
   To court my new jo."
"Master, though the night be merk,
   I'se follow through the snow.

"Court her, master, court her,
   So shall ye do weel;
But and ben she'll guide the house,
   I'se get milk and meal.
Ye'se get lilting while she sits
   With her rock and reel."

"For, oh! she has a sweet tongue,
   And een that look down,
A gold girdle for her waist,
   And a purple gown.
She has a good word forbye
   Fra a' folk in the town."

" Court her, master, court her,
So shall ye do weel."

LIKE A LAVEROCK IN THE LIFT.

IT'S we two, it's we two, it's we two for aye,
    All the world and we two, and Heaven be our stay.
Like a laverock in the lift, sing, O bonny bride!
All the world was Adam once, with Eve by his side.

What's the world, my lass, my love!—what can it do?
I am thine, and thou art mine; life is sweet and new.
If the world have missed the mark, let it stand by,
For we two have gotten leave, and once more we'll try.

Like a laverock in the lift, sing, O bonny bride!
It's we two, it's we two, happy side by side.
Take a kiss from me thy man; now the song begins:
"All is made afresh for us, and the brave heart wins."

When the darker days come, and no sun will shine,
Thou shalt dry my tears, lass, and I'll dry thine.
It's we two, it's we two, while the world's away,
Sitting by the golden sheaves on our wedding-day.

AT ONE AGAIN.

41

AT ONE AGAIN.

I. NOONDAY.

TWO angry men — in heat they sever,
    And one goes home by a harvest field : —
" Hope's nought," quoth he, "and vain endeavour :
    " I said and say it, I will not yield !

" As for this wrong, no art can mend it,
    The bond is shiver'd that held us twain :
Old friends we be, but law must end it,
    Whether for loss or whether for gain.

"*His strawberry cow slipped loose her tether,*
And trod the best of my barley down."

At One Again.

"Yon stream is small — full slow its wending ;
  But winning is sweet, but right is fine ;
And shoal of trout, or willowy bending —
  Though Law be costly — I'll prove them mine.

" His strawberry cow slipped loose her tether,
  And trod the best of my barley down ;
His little lasses at play together
  Pluck'd the poppies my boys had grown.

" What then ? — Why nought ! *She* lack'd of reason :
  And *they* — my little ones match them well : —
But *this* — Nay all things have their season,
  And 'tis my season to curb and quell."

II. SUNSET.

So saith he, when noontide fervours flout him,
  So thinks, when the West is amber and red,
When he smells the hop-vines sweet about him,
  And the clouds are rosy overhead.

While slender and tall the hop-poles going
  Straight to the West in their leafy lines,
Portion it out into chambers, glowing,
  And bask in red day as the sun declines.

Between the leaves in his latticed arbour
  He sees the sky, as they flutter and turn,
While moor'd like boats in a golden harbour
  The fleets of feathery cloudlets burn.

At One Again.

Withdrawn in shadow, he thinketh over
  Harsh thoughts, the fruit-laden trees among,
Till pheasants call their young to cover,
  And cushats coo them a nursery song.

And flocks of ducks forsake their sedges,
  Wending home to the wide barn-door,
And loaded wains between the hedges
  Slowly creep to his threshing floor —

Slowly creep.   And his tired senses,
  Float him over the magic stream,
To a world where Fancy recompenses
  Vengeful thoughts, with a troubled dream !

" *And his tired senses,*
Float him over the magic stream."

III. THE DREAM.

WHAT'S this? a wood — What's that? one calleth,
    Calleth and cryeth in mortal dread —
He hears men strive — then somewhat falleth! —
    "Help me, neighbour — I'm hard bestead."

The dream is strong — the voice he knoweth —
    But when he would run, his feet are fast,
And death lies beyond, and no man goeth
    To help, and he says the time is past.

His feet are held, and he shakes all over, —
    Nay — they are free — he has found the place —
Green boughs are gather'd — what is't they cover? —
    "I pray you, look on the dead man's face:

48

At One Again.

You that stand by," he saith, and cowers —
  "Man, or Angel, to guard the dead
With shadowy spear, and a brow that lowers,
  And wing-points reared in the gloom o'erhead. —

I dare not look. He wronged me never.
  Men say we differ'd ; they speak amiss :
This man and I were neighbours ever —
  I would have ventured my life for his.

But fast my feet were — fast with tangles —
  Aye ! words — but they were not sharp, I trow,
Though parish feuds and vestry wrangles —
  O pitiful sight — I see thee now ! —

If we fell out, 'twas but foul weather,
  After long shining ! O bitter cup, —
What — dead ? — why, man, we play'd together —
  Art dead — ere a friend can make it up ? "

IV. THE WAKING.

OVER his head the chafer hummeth,
    Under his feet shut daisies bend:
Waken, man! the enemy cometh,
    Thy neighbour, counted so long a friend.

He cannot waken — and firm, and steady,
    The enemy comes with lowering brow;
He looks for war, his heart is ready,
    His thoughts are bitter — he will not bow.

He fronts the seat, — the dream is flinging
    A spell that his footsteps may not break, —
But one in the garden of hops is singing —
    The dreamer hears it, and starts awake.

"But one in the garden of hops is singing —
The dreamer hears it, and starts awake."

V. A SONG.

WALKING apart, she thinks none listen ;
　　And now she carols, and now she stops ;
And the evening star begins to glisten
　　Atween the lines of blossoming hops.

Sweetest Mercy, your mother taught you
　　All uses and cares that to maids belong ;
Apt scholar to read and to sew she thought you —
　　She did not teach you that tender song —

" The lady sang in her charmèd bower,
　　Sheltered and safe under roses blown —
' *Storm cannot touch me, hail, nor shower,*
　　Where all alone I sit, all alone.

" *The lady sang in her charmèd bower,*
Sheltered and safe under roses blown."

At One Again.

My bower! The fair Fay twined it round me;
Care nor trouble can pierce it through;
But once a sigh from the warm world found me
Between two leaves that were bent with dew.

And day to night, and night to morrow,
Though soft as slumber the long hours wore
I looked for my dower of love, of sorrow —
Is there no more — no more — no more?'

Give her the sun-sweet light, and duly
  To walk in shadow, nor chide her part ;
Give her the rose, and truly, truly —
  To wear its thorn with a patient heart. —

Misty as dreams the moonbeam lyeth
  Chequered and faint on her charmèd floor ;
The lady singeth, the lady sigheth —
  ' Is there no more — no more — no more !' "

VI. LOVERS.

A CRASH of boughs!—one through them breaking!
　　Mercy is startled, and fain would fly,
But e'en as she turns, her steps o'ertaking,
　　He pleads with her—" Mercy, it is but I !"

" Mercy !" he touches her hand unbidden—
　　" The air is balmy, I pray you stay—
Mercy ? " Her downcast eyes are hidden,
　　And never a word she has to say.

Till closer drawn, her prison'd fingers
　　He takes to his lips with a yearning strong ;
And she murmurs low, that late she lingers,
　　Her mother will want her, and think her long.

At One Again.

"Good mother is she, then honour duly
  The lightest wish in her heart that stirs ;
But there is a bond yet dearer truly,
  And there is a love that passeth hers.

Mercy, Mercy!" Her heart attendeth —
  Love's birthday blush on her brow lies sweet ;
She turns her face when his own he bendeth,
  And the lips of the youth and the maiden meet.

"*She turns her face when his own he bendeth,*
And the lips of the youth and the maiden meet."

VII. FATHERS.

MOVE through the bowering hops, O lovers,—
    Wander down to the golden West,—
But two stand mute in the shade that covers
    Your love and youth from their souls opprest.

A little shame on their spirits stealing,—
    A little pride that is loth to sue,—
A little struggle with soften'd feeling,—
    And a world of fatherly care for you.

One says: "To this same running water,
    May be, Neighbour, your claim is best."
And one — "Your son has kissed my daughter:
    Let the matters between us — rest."

"*Move through the bowering hops, O lovers,* —
Wander down to the golden West."